O, RILEY O'SMILEY

Written and illustrated by

Todd Aaron Smith

A Division of Thomas Nelson Publishers
Since 1798

www.thomasnelson.com

Library of Congress Cataloging-in-Publication Data
Smith, Todd Aaron.
    Riley O'Smiley / Todd Aaron Smith.
        p. cm.
    Summary: When he is mistaken for a sea monster, Riley O'Smiley
secretly rescues the people who have come to capture him, and
thanks God for making him just as he is, able to help others even
when they do not know he is there.
    ISBN-10: 1-4003-0818-6
    ISBN-13: 978-1-4003-0818-7
    [1. Helpfulness—Fiction. 2. Sea monsters—Fiction. 3. Conduct
of life—Fiction.] I. Title.
PZ7.S6596Ril 2006
[E]-dc22
                                            2005038004

Printed in China
06 07 08 09 10 LEO 5 4 3 2

"Lord, you have made many things.
With your wisdom you made them all.
The earth is full of your riches.
Look at the sea, so big and wide.
Its creatures large and small cannot be counted.
Ships travel over the ocean.
And there is the sea monster Leviathan,
which you made to play there."
PSALM 104:24—26

TV news reporters stood near the edge of the water. Bright lights shined. Cameras clicked. Papers shuffled.

"Good morning. This is Monica for News Channel 7 reporting to you live from the banks of this beautiful coastline! Thousands of travelers come here each year to fish and sail these waters."

Suddenly, a big blue creature popped up out of
the water behind her. Riley O'Smiley peeked over
Monica's shoulder to get a better look!

Riley was from a long line of O'Smileys. When he
saw the camera, he couldn't help but smile. After all,
being smiley is what all O'Smileys do best!

"AAAAAGGGGHHHHH!" screamed Monica.

But Riley O'Smiley kept being smiley. *What a funny game!* he laughed. Just for fun Riley yelled back, "AAAGGGHHH!"

Papers went flying. Cameras fell over. Everyone started running!

Soon all the people who had watched the newscast wanted to come see the big sea creature. "Where is that monster we saw on TV?" they asked.

Before long Riley O'Smiley was famous. Stores were stocked with toys, magazines, and just about everything that looked like Riley.

Other news reporters began crowding around Monica. "What kind of creature is this?" and "Where did he go?" they kept asking.

Although nobody had actually seen him since that first day, Riley O'Smiley could see the crowds. He even saw a giant billboard that read *Come Visit the Amazing Sea Monster*. He had never seen such a big picture of himself before.

COME VISIT THE AMAZING SEA MONSTER

Many families came to the famous beach. "Take my picture right here," said one little boy. "This is right where the sea monster was!"

Riley O'Smiley thought it was all pretty silly, really.

But not everyone was so smiley about Riley. Some reporters began to say Riley wasn't real. "He's only a large duck!" others said. Some even said it was all just a big joke or trick photography.

It was hard to tell what had actually happened since the news clip was so blurry. Experts watched the video over and over again to figure out what kind of animal Riley O'Smiley was. They took Riley's measurements and compared every animal—from ducks to dinosaurs—to his image.

Most people didn't really care what Riley was.
But everyone wanted to be the first to find him!

They set sail the next morning for the open sea.
Finally the ships stopped, and divers jumped into
the murky water to find the creature.

Uh oh! thought Riley, who was now not so smiley. Riley could see the divers. He saw their cameras and flashlights. But there was more in the water than just Riley O'Smiley and the divers. . . .

SHARKS!

And they were getting closer and closer to the divers! Riley knew this wasn't good. So he did what he did best. He popped up between the sharks and the divers and gave his great big smile.

The sharks were *not* smiley. They were scared! Even they had heard about this creature of the sea. And they swam away as quickly as they could.

The divers never knew Riley O'Smiley saved their lives. Instead, they just kept trying to capture him.

"The fog is too thick. Let's head back to shore, men,"
said the man who smelled like fresh suntan lotion.
But the diver at the front of the ship yelled back,
"The lighthouse isn't working! There's no light,
and I can't hear the foghorn!"

Riley watched the men trying to guess their
way through the fog. But Riley knew they were
dangerously close to the sharp, jagged rocks. *Those
people are in trouble,* Riley thought, *I've got to help!*

God had made Riley O'Smiley with an amazing
fiery breath. And he knew just what to do. Quickly
he breathed fire into the sky. It was like a great
fireworks show! No one had ever seen anything
like it.

"What on earth is that?" a sailor called out.
The men were puzzled. "Slow down the boats!"
they cried.

Next, Riley tilted back his head. He belted out the loudest "RRRRROOOOAAARRR!" he'd ever made. The boats stopped. The men looked. At last they saw how close to land they really were. "I don't know what made that noise, but it saved our lives!" they said to each other. Riley was smiley again.

Riley O'Smiley quietly disappeared beneath the
water, and the boats safely reached the shore.
While unloading the boats, one man stopped to
look out at the big ocean. "You suppose there
really is a great sea monster out there?" he asked.
"Who knows?" replied his friend. "If there is,
we'll find him one day."

As Riley swam deeper into the ocean, he knew it didn't matter what anyone else thought. Riley O'Smiley knew he was real. *Thank You, God,* Riley smiled, *for making me just like You did!*

So remember Riley O'Smiley's story, and don't forget that God is taking care of you— even when you don't know He is doing it.